This Little Tiger book belongs to:

_____

_____

_____

For Moth, Jennifer and Hannah xx ~ B D

For Fin and Luke, my favourite Phews ~ E L

LITTLE TIGER PRESS LTD,
an imprint of the Little Tiger Group
1 Coda Studios, 189 Munster Road, London SW6 6AW
Imported into the EEA by Penguin Random House Ireland,
Morrison Chambers, 32 Nassau Street, Dublin D02 YH68
www.littletiger.co.uk

First published in Great Britain 2020
This edition published 2020

Text by Becky Davies
Illustrations by Emma Levey
Text and illustrations copyright © Little Tiger Press Ltd 2020

A CIP catalogue record for this book is available from
the British Library

Printed in China • LTP/1400/4010/0621

2 4 6 8 10 9 7 5 3

DON'T Mess with DUCK!

Becky Davies
&
Emma Leney

LITTLE TIGER

LONDON

Duck was the grumpiest bird in the whole pond. He liked peace. He liked quiet. And he liked to be left alone.

But Duck's neighbours liked flapping.

They liked quacking.

And they really liked . . .

. . . Splashing!

"Bleurgh!"

"You birds wouldn't know peace if it bit you on the bottoms," said Duck. "I'm off to find somewhere QUIET!"

With that, he grabbed his suitcase and squelched away.

Duck hadn't waddled far when he found a new pond. There wasn't a noisy duck in sight! Time for some serious relaxing.

"Ahhhhh," he sighed happily. "Now THIS is perfect."

But then . . .

Boom,

Boom,

Boom!

"Drat!"

Suddenly, it wasn't.

The next pond was packed with singers.

"Clear off!"

And the one after that was full of swimmers!

Duck was going to have to get clever.

Duck waddled all the way to the big city.
He found a fancy fountain . . .

But it wasn't peaceful.

So Duck trekked all the way up the tall mountain.
He found a steaming spring . . .

But it wasn't private. Not private at all!

Then Duck went all the way down to the deep caves.
And the pond he found there . . .

. . . was DEFINITELY no good!

"EEEEEEEK!"

At last – AT LAST! Duck
found another pond.
    "Could it be the one?"
he gasped.

Quiet? Tick.
Peaceful? Tick!

Not too shabby for Duck!
Not too shabby at all.

"Ahhhh," he sighed happily. Alone at last.

"Ahhhh," echoed
another voice in the reeds.

Duck wasn't alone after all. A very small, very grumpy frog blinked up at him.

"Clear off!" they both said.

Duck gave Frog his grumpiest glare.
It was FIERCE. It was FEROCIOUS!
But Frog glared right back!
"This is my pond," said Frog.
"Stay out of my way."
"It's MY pond!" said Duck.
"And you stay out of MY way!"

So they each did just that.

Duck fished, quietly.

And Frog gardened, quietly.

Duck read.

Frog painted.

And they both took naps in the sunshine. Duck found that living with Frog was surprisingly . . . nice.

But the peace and quiet didn't last long.

One day, Duck was enjoying an early morning swim when . . .

Thud!

Thud!

Thud!

He was rudely interrupted.
"Frog!" Duck shouted. "Keep it down!"

On the other side of the pond, Frog was pruning
the reeds when another . . .

Thud!

Thud!

Thud!

. . . ruined his concentration entirely.
"Duck!" Frog bellowed. "Be QUIET!"
They were both about to yell "SHUSH!" when . . .

"Timber!"

called a jolly beaver
from the bank.

"Yikes!"

"Kids, come say hi!" beamed Beaver. "When we get the dam finished you'll be our new neighbours."

Neighbours?

Duck and Frog narrowed their eyes. They took a deep breath. They started to say "CLEAR OFF!" But then they looked at each other.

Duck very much liked peace. And Frog very much liked quiet.
But sharing the pond had been almost . . . better.
Duck realised that this grumpy little frog was now his friend,
and that he knew just what to say to the beavers . . .

"Welcome to our pond!"